In Loving Memory of my daughter.
Leah Elizabeth Carter.
January 22, 1999- December 31, 2018

CAN YOU SEE ME?

Written by Laura Mccarty

Illustrated by Allyson Graves

Tyler is eight years old, and lives with his parents, his older brother Tim, and little sister Tess.

Tyler's brother Tim is thirteen, and is a really good football player.

His sister Tess, is a cute little two year old, and is just learning to talk.

Tyler is usually quiet, because it can
be pretty chaotic at home, with his
brother having football
practice and games,

as well as Tess getting into
everything! She has to be
watched by everyone.

At school, Tyler makes good grades, and always follows the rules. He never gets into trouble, or talks when the "no talking rule is on." Tyler gets along with everyone.

He has a few friends he talks to, but he is very shy, and sort of blends in with the others.

One afternoon, Tyler came home from school, and his parents were so happy. Tim had won a trophy for scoring the most touchdowns in the last game.

They put a picture of him with his trophy on the refrigerator. Tyler was happy for him, but he wished he could "do something good," or "make his parents proud."

That night at supper, Tess started saying some new words. The whole family clapped, and his parents started taking pictures. They were so excited!

Tyler started wondering if he was ever going to be noticed, or make his parents proud.

He thought, "I'm not the good ball player, or the cute baby. I'm just Tyler, plain and unnoticed."

At school one day, there was a fire drill, where everyone leaves the room in an orderly fashion, to practice in case there were to be a real fire. Each student lined up according to where their seats were.

As Tyler got out of his seat, he started thinking about Carla, a girl in his class, who has to use braces to walk. He went back to her desk, took her by the arm, and helped her out of the building, where the class was to meet.

No one else had offered to help her. Mrs. Baker, Tyler's teacher, had not asked him to help. Tyler just started thinking that "someone will need to help Carla."

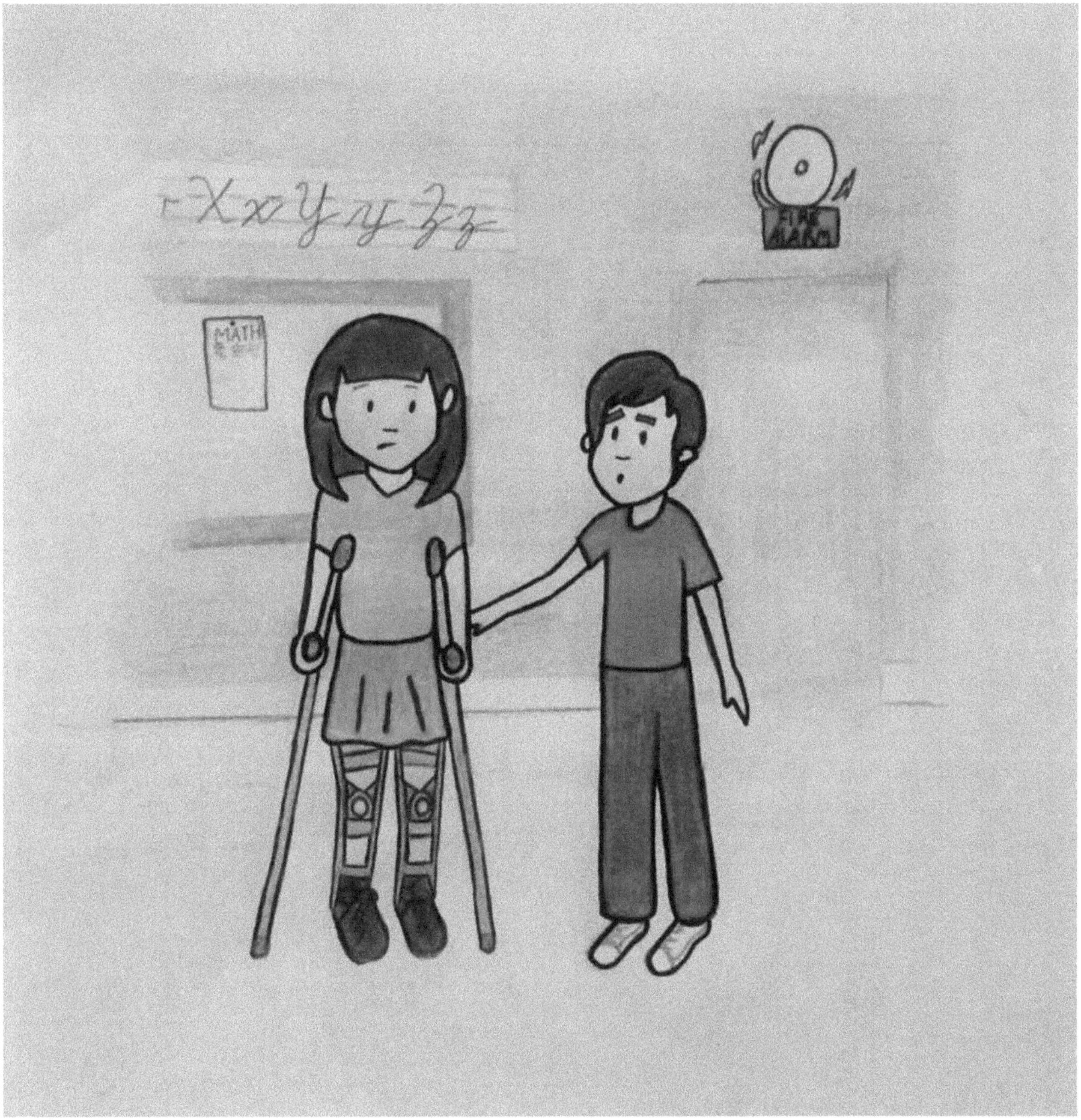
Xx Yy Zz
MATH
FIRE ALARM

That afternoon the class played a game, and teams were chosen. Each student raised their hand and said,

"pick me!" "pick me"!

Tyler raised his hand but was quiet, and not noticed by the leaders. He was not chosen, and he felt so sad, and left out. After the game, they had a restroom break.

Tyler couldn't hold back the tears. He put his head on his desk and cried. Mrs. Baker saw Tyler was still in his seat while everyone else was out playing.

Mrs. Baker went over to him, and asked
"What's wrong Tyler? Are you sick?"

He raised his head and said, "Nobody ever notices me.
I don't think anyone will ever see me."

Mrs. Baker said, "Who doesn't see you?"

"Everybody," said Tyler, "Momma and daddy only see what Tim and Tess do. The other kids don't pick me. I don't think they will ever notice me."

Tyler continued to cry, and Mrs. Baker said, "Tyler look at me."

He raised his head, and she started wiping his tears. Mrs. Baker said "Tyler, I see you all of the time. I see you when you wait in line, without pushing or shoving. I see you when you say please and thank you. I see you share and follow all of the rules. I also saw you help Carla leave the room during the fire drill. Do you know how kind and thoughtful that was?"

Tyler thought about what Mrs. Baker had said.

He replied, "You mean you see me?"

"Of course I do," said Mrs. Baker, "You are one the best students in this class. I don't always say your name, because I don't have to. You're so smart and respectful. I never have to remind you. Sometimes, we don't always say the names of the quiet, respectful students, but we appreciate them. Tyler, I always notice you."

The kind comments Mrs. Baker made, had helped Tyler to feel better. He couldn't believe she saw him helping Carla, or when he's following the rules.

Tyler started to smile and then he asked, Mrs. Baker, "Do you think my parents notice me?"

"Of course they do! They know what a good son and brother you are! They just get busy, but they love you."

Then Mrs. Baker patted him on the back, as the other students were coming back into the room. Tyler felt so much better the rest of the day.

That afternoon before school ended, Mrs. Baker made an announcement. "I want to present this certificate for

"Outstanding Citizenship"

to one of you, for excellent behavior and thinking of others.

"This award goes to Tyler Evans."

The whole class started clapping, and Tyler was shocked, as he went up to get his certificate.

Tyler had never been cheered for or recognized for anything. He smiled and thanked Mrs. Baker.

As Tyler walked in the door at home, he couldn't wait to show his award to his parents. He ran to his mother and said,

"Look what I got today!"

Tyler's mom hugged him, and said, **"That's great!"**

Then she called his daddy, and brother to see what Tyler had achieved. His daddy and Tim both hugged and congratulated him.

Then Tyler's momma put the award on the refrigerator with Tim and Tess's things.

Tyler felt so proud, and he said to his parents, "I'm so happy you all have noticed me."

Tyler's momma and daddy knelt down and hugged him.

His momma told him, "Tyler we always notice you! You are our sweet and smart son. We're always proud of you."

"You are, replied Tyler? I didn't know you saw me, just Tim and Tess."

Tyler's mom hugged him again and said,
"We see you all of the time. You are a sweet,
loving son. Always remember that we see you and will
always be proud of who you are."

Tyler felt happy inside, and then told his parents,
"I notice you all too, so I guess I am important,
by just being me."

Disclaimer Last updated: March 11th, 2020

The information contained in this book is for the purpose of children's reading & enjoyment only. Laura McCarty and Backwoods Books assumes no responsibility for errors or omissions in the contents on the Service. In no event shall Backwoods Books or Laura McCarty be liable for any special, direct, indirect, consequential, or incidental damages or any damages whatsoever, whether in an action of contract, negligence or other tort, arising out of or in connection with the use of the Service or the contents of the Service.

Backwoods Books and Laura McCarty reserve the right to make additions, deletions, or modification to the contents on the Service at any time without prior notice.

CPSIA information can be obtained
at www.ICGtesting.com
Printed in the USA
BVHW022302300421
606212BV00004B/357